LOVE

IN THE

PROMISED

LAND

By

Shrawan Thapa

You might feel tired,

Exhausted,

hurt maybe,

but you are not that,

you are a champ.

Table of Contents

x

Ocean of love

A thousand rivers make a sea,

One thousand memories;

Makes love seen.

It starts with just a stream,

Maybe just a Hello!

Love, later screams.

Rivers flow from all directions,

But the ocean stays,

Calm and peaceful.

For love, it carries, of all the rivers,

For all the pain it takes in,

This is not love.

This is the "Ocean of love."

Love that thousands sing about it,

Love that everyone desires.

Love so deep, nobody can skip.

Who are you?

You came this late

Only to rescue

I hope I don't screw

Dark

Dark! dark, darkness arises;

On this night, my soul was scary bright.

Dark! dark, darkness from left to right

Soul consuming into the night

This void, swallowing my sanity

Dark! dark, darkness moves in my mind

Spreading darkness all over my veins

Pumps poison; my heart dead.

Devil and Angel

Met in a place unlikely,

But pleasant they felt.

Beauty like her, he couldn't resist but approach.

She was quite shy at first, but he was consistent.

She was an angel. He was a devil.

She resented and pushed him as much as she could.

But the devil had her eventually. She felt.

The goodness of her soul, the warmth of her, melts his heart like snow.

Oh! he got one too.

The devil is no devil anymore

Such a changed man, he felt.

He felt she was the answer to all his prayers.

Now they both worship and love each other.

Such a love forever would be shameful.

Damn! I envy writing such a pleasant story.

My angel

Like an angel bright,

She came into my life

Killed the demons dark!

Erased the fears surrounding my heart

Dark! Dark, what dark?

Look! There she stands, with her bright heart.

What's on your mind?

It's safe; it's me.

Show me your face,

Tell me your truth.

Let me know,

What do you enjoy?

What's fun for you?

How's your heaven?

You were the best thing that ever happened to me.

So humble, kind, and sweet, the one I ever got to know.

It pains to think about losing you

It may sound different; I've planned for us over a few years already.

If it's only a day until I live,

I want to keep talking with you.

Tell me what you love and dislike about me

Let me know

what should be done a little more and less.

Which are your chapters?

Let me read you line by line.

I'll tear all the pages of pain and sorrows.

I wanna fill the remaining ones with lots of fun,

I promise.

I keep reliving the moments with you, chatting and
seeing you for the first time.

If I had a wish,

I would only ask to go back in time and

fix things between us.

I would trade anything for that moment to come back.

I believe life is a box of chocolates.

I only want the best!

Let's keep going, not past but forward

Making mistakes is foolish of me;

that only makes me wiser.

I believe in making mistakes;

never repeat one, I'll promise.

A poet's love

I wanna bore you with my poems,

And pour you a warm cup of coffee,

Hold you till my last breath,

Love you till my heart beats.

This is a selfless love

As it goes

So does my love flow

From my heart

Into yours

The warmth

We exchange

Bodies? No

Souls we intertwine

Limits we cross

Boundaries we break

All this love

We embrace

Night and morning

This life and next

We march ahead

There we merge

Like two rivers

Big strong, us

Let's flow in this wind,

As love flows to the owns.

Do you see me in your sweet dreams?

Sweet sleep, baby sleep

Your smile: baby's smile

Your laughter, like a rainbow after

Pleasant dream: a dream of me, of you

On a hill, mountain and caves

Hidden lakes, rivers and forest

Sweet babe on your face,

I see my future traced!

Will you not rest?

For I wait; in our dream place.

You can find me here

Come, find me.

Running into your arms.

Come close,

And close your eyes!

Shut down your fears,

Let go of those tears!

Can't you see,

That I'm here?

My bleeding heart in your broken jar of promise

Stories as old as trees, blown by the tides of time

Eroding strength and fading memories on the way

Rests on me as it is.

She speaks in riddles,

It makes my heart tickle,

And her soft fingers,

Plays miseries on my heartstring.

Who is he?

Deep, mysterious, sophisticated.

He may not be your usual cup of tea,

But remember, he's unique.

You say, what could he feel?

When you only met once,

Rarely texted; just recently,

And started sharing personal stuff.

A hard shell to crack, though.

He loves to keep his feelings to himself.

Trying to understand might be difficult too.

Feels great to talk with someone with similar views, don't you?

You still say, how could he?

Well! Don't you feel something?

He thinks of you sometimes and wonders what you two could be.

It's not that he doesn't feel the way you are guessing, but it's different with you.

He believes life is a journey, taking it slowly and enjoying every piece bit by bit.

He is a curious fella, but he'll give you space as promised.

Just remind him of your boundary, and he'll respect it.

Now, tell me. What do you think of him?

What she said

She says you look good,

Your voice is cute.

You are so hot,

You are a stud.

She keeps teasing,

Keeps pleasing.

All about her

She looks at me thirsty,

Makes me feel twenty.

Never stops talking,

The conversations don't get boring.

She is pretty awesome,

Not perfect but feels perfect.

Alone on the loves' island

All his life, he felt unlovable and unworthy of love until her.

He shared his vulnerabilities and his weaknesses.

He loves her and waits for her to feel the same way.

With all the sunlight in the day sky,

He only sees her.

All his thoughts, today and tomorrow, are hers.

She is irresistible.

Even in his dreams, she becomes irreplaceable.

All her traces everywhere, in everyone he meets.

He wants to be with her in all the Joys and sorrows.

He wants her to know she has his back in all her battles.

He will wait until she feels the same.

First love

It was her eyes

When I saw.

I knew that

She was mine

Mine to keep

Mine forever

Mine to save

Until I breathe

Is this love?

Was it her warm hugs?

Or those cute smiles?

Was it those sweet voices?

Those early morning texts or

Late-night calls?

100 missed calls?

Do I call it love?

What is Love?

Love is a beautiful feeling,

It is the nature of healing.

We fall in love, we grow in love

We see the real world with love.

It is holy. It is pure

It is fun, and it is sure

Don't be afraid to love,

Be afraid to lose.

Don't be shy to express yourself,

Be shy to hide.

If you love, then you do care,

If you care, then you do share,

If you share, then you don't fear,

If you don't worry, then you do cheer,

If you do cheer, then you are near.

To love or hate, the choice is yours,

Always remember, the consequences then follow.

When you smiled like the sun, and I watched you like a sunflower

As sparkling as your soul is,

So is your smile.

Whenever I think of you,

Your smiling face is all I see.

Believe me, when I say; tù es muy bonito

Mi amigo, you are frank and cool.

I can't stop thinking of your face,

Since we met,

Now you play all the love beats on my heart's string.

The unhappening

Strangers-Strangers, not for long,

Conversations all day long.

Sweet talks and laughs

She: knew not he was in love.

He: thought she knew,

Maybe she was in love.

But not; she had a guy.

To her, he was just another guy!

He: Feeling used, decides not to talk.

She: like an old friend, came back again.

His heart: like snow, melted before the sun.

In every girl he meets, he sees you!

How could he say;

When she was with somebody else?

Later, she called him a good friend.

Then he knew;

All this pain; was just in vain.

So many tears all these years!

What should he do to deserve her?

When you can't be mine

You look lovely!

You look lovely,

My heart aches.

You sound funny!

You sound funny,

Now my heart breaks.

Do you love me?

Do you love me?

Now my handshakes.

A song of a broken heart

My heart bleeds poison.

Feels no pain;

I keep moving in this forest-dense,

Darkness, while it spreads, in my veins.

The horrified mind blasts the terrifying bombs of
anxiety and agony.

Dry. My soul feels like a desert.

My eyes, all drained, only see the rain.

The mind keeps moving.

The heart bleeding; can't stop this,

I can't stop this pain.

My heart can't stop bleeding:

Bleeding poison inside me.

I could sew it if it were torn,

If broken, I could mend it,

But my heart is bleeding;

There's no tape or glue to fix it,

No medicine can cure this disease.

Mental warfare

The air was too heavy to breathe,
Sun; too hot to stand

Life; restless to be calming
Happiness, misplaced in a race,

Introverted to be outgoing,
Reserved; to open up

Confused to take a step,
No hope of carrying on.

Nothing to look back at,
No memories.

Nothing to cry for,
Nobody to miss.

Empty voices,
Shout words loud.

How I killed myself in the mind-place

Broke are my wings. I can fly no more.

Broken are my legs. They walk no more.

Eyes so blind, it only sees red

The heart bleeding in.

The mind can't stop screaming,

Blind, my eyes see dark: only darkness,

I could see the light if you'll bring

Though I can't see; I can't see,

For I'm blind. You see?

Too many deaths. I see

While it bringeth upon me

Too much pain;

The heart is still bleeding.

I'm bleeding in too much pain

Too much pain; I bleed in vain

So much pain, I can't lend

Only so much blood I can drain.

Dreams running wild:

No birds here fly,

No sweet songs, they sing.

In this valley of death, I hear only the screams.

This is it, is it?

The devil cries with tears in his eyes.

But the angel of death kisses my forehead.

With joy in her eyes,

She sings sweet melodies of goodbyes.

Holding my hand;

She says, "It is time you come home.

My child, come home.

Thy father awaits at the dinner table.

Thy mother has cooked your favourite meal.

Thy plate is already filled.

Come home, child, she says to me."

I feel cold inside

The boiling heat of the atmosphere,

Couldn't even warm the ice inside!

Surrounded by all this love,

With all this knowledge,

I still feel empty.

Soul constantly searching for deeper meaning

Mind trying to figure how

Everything is still here inside this body,

but where do I exist?

Like a decaying leaf, I feel all dead inside.

In this quest to discover myself, I lost myself
somewhere along the way.

After all the burns to my heart,

it feels no pain, nothing! Nothing at all.

I'm afraid I've been an abandoned

cold iron chair in the rain.

You won't understand. No,

you can't feel my pain, but you could listen to

The stories of the battles in the war of survival

You will always find me

 on the frontline with me and myself.

Who am I?

I'm the battleship. I'm the cannon

The horse and the horseman,

The sword and the swordsman

The arrow and the bow

The country and its king

It's all me.

I'm infected and also the disease;

I'm living and the dying

I'm the poet, and the poem

I'm the writer and the story

I'm among the living and the dead.

I'm the best day and the worse nightmare;

I'm the yin and the yang

I'm the peace and the war

I'm the still hills and the tall trees

I'm the river, and its fish

I'm all the glory of the battlefield,

And the one running away from it.

 I'm the kind one here,

Also, the cruellest of them all.

I'm the killer and the healer.

I'm the mind and the soul.

I'm the heart and its love.

I'm the work and sweat.

I'm the story and its narrator

I'm the deep roots and the branches

I'm the sweet breeze and the storm

I'm the bright sky and the rain

I've died several times,

Been defeated to fight another day.

I've been telling these tales of my life,

The never-ending cycles of my life,

The repetitive games that lie,

Like days and nights,

A rotating clock.

I only start for it to end,

And end just to start.

I loved,

and been loyal, yet betrayed.

I've been optimistic; scared as well.

I've trained and failed.

I've been on the winning side and the other side.

I may not completely understand how this world works,

But I certainly know my world, one inside me—the
untouched beauties and colours hidden

and protected within.

Inch by inch, I progress

Bucket by bucket, I throw the sorrows that have been
drowning me

Chapter by chapter, I keep writing,

Writing the incomplete story of my only life.

Emptiness

With a broken heart, bare hands,

And empty pocket,

I have nothing to give.

I can't accept it,

What I don't deserve.

With my drenched heart,

I come to your kingdom,

In hopes of love.

A letter to the supreme creator

Dear Lord,

Take me to paradise.

All the beautiful flowers to see,

Pleasant music and feast,

To the place of truth and eternal peace.

Take me to my lord.

Oh! I'll praise him,

I'll thank him for this gift;

This holy eternal love,

How do I share?

Oh! I want to share,

My brothers and sisters are in despair.

Save me, my lord.

The devil always knocks at my door.

With the sounds of terror that I don't see

The caged animal is roaring to break free.

My burdened soul seeks relief.

Fill the jar of my life; with your love and bliss.

Take me to his feet;

The only place, I believe.

The games of human life

Quenching draining mind into understanding mine

Cleaning filth of thought

Fighting the wrath of manipulations and lies

Heat of tyranny

Temptations of reality

Reality of Fantasy

Fantasy of you

Reading faces, the ones hidden

Listening to the voices inside the voice

Counting infinite to infinite

Looking beyond the blues of the sky

Diving inside the earth itself!

Lost in the puzzles of life,

Sleeping longer than the nights,

Seeing behind these starry lights.

I was in paradise

Chill winds blow,

Through the shiny mountains,

Rivers, lakes, waterfalls,

And tempting green forests,

They call it a wonderland.

Ego death

As the sun melts the snow,

Love melts our ego.

Always the sun comes,

Touching every one with its rays, warm.

When eyes are on the light,

The shadow gets lost.

All the earthly problems,

Seems insignificant now.

This is heaven

The sun, the moon, the clouds, and the rain is all here

The quietness of the mind,

The delightful healing of nature,

Unread tales of an unknown place,

This mystery prevails through the ages.

Deep blue ocean,

Tall white mountains,

Are uncountable captivating smiles of nature.

Sweet goodbyes,

To an extraordinary site,

A divine culture and a delicious delight.

Dreams divine

Like every day, I woke up in my dream

Life half-lived dreams unfulfilled

Staying in this agony,

Far away I go to find me

Lost on the echoes of 21st-century

Modern man, they call me

Kindness and humanity when I see

Hopeful and surprised, I am

What a world we live in

Is it just a dream or my reality

Oh, the universe comes into my dream

The other half of my life begin

What I see, I believe

Treasuring the humanity

Walking upon the dead bodies

I march forward like a soldier of God

Commander of the living, they call me

We reach the gates of heaven,

Beautiful palace far away we see,

"Come with me, child," our mother sings,

Brothers and sisters rejoice with joy.

Such a bright smile, my eyes turned blind.

But I see now.

I see the truth,

I see the Lord.

After all, it was but a test

And now we can pass through!

Divinity

Find me, o Lord, bind me by your feet

Hold me in your heart

That is where I'm supposed to be

For eternity, I have wanted this

What a human life I lived!

Yesterday, blues

Sometimes just out of the blue, I miss old me

Old friends, old dreams, and good old days

The happy child that's quiet now

Always smiling face is now just a mask

All these manufactured emotions are so confusing.

Why can't this be normal, just simple as it used to be?

The little cat

Lying on that roof

The sweet little cat.

Sings the "meow-meow-mew."

Red, the sun

Warms its belly,

The puffy-puffy cat,

Sleeps in a muse.

Those sweet little eyes,

What colours do they see,

Into the deep blue,

when do they look?

Smiling, smiling!

The old little cat,

With its kittens too,

Sings the "meow-meow-mew."

The oceanic blue

Into the deep sky

There I see

When I look,

The oceanic blue!

Dear Anna

The day we met,

Lost in the forest,

I found you,

Passing a torch,

We walk ahead to the top

The forest was dark and deep

But we have a place to be

Can't rest here, said thee

For thy Lord, I seek

How can I rest? While this darkness spreads!

With all the universe in our hearts

We share joy, and we see smiles on each other's faces

Our souls are so bright, darkness goes trembling blind

Love. Holy and pure, she found her own

Now she lights many candles

With joy,

She is finally home.

She was lost

Aren't we all?

Day

What a beautiful day,

Rest here, oh my pretty head

Laugh more and stay a while

What a pleasant surprise that would be,

Nights

This lonely night took me away,

Away from my sight.

Lovely it is, what I see,

Melodies of sleep. Sweet.

Now I'm here, but I'm nobody.

I'm here and everywhere

I'm everybody.

Lost in the modern echoes but still

Hear my soul calling

Keep quiet! I tell my mind

All these unusual, unfinished tales it sings

What excitement and what misery it brings.

But I want to sleep; give me my peace

Doors of heaven

Do you know what the doors of heaven are made of?

Oh, dear!

Living in this generation, we have been so used to building walls and strong doors to hide our insecurities and fears!

Do you think there are doors in heaven?

There is no fear at God's home

No insecurities, no walls to hide

It's only love there,

No one needs to fear;

For God's kingdom is nearby.

Counting love until you say yes!

The difficult hundred words to choose

Ten thousand, I wish to say

In this silence, we exchange;

The longest texts.

One word equals a thousand wishes,

And your three words;

With millions of feelings,

I take to my heartache

Building love higher than Everest

I'm writing my heart,

As a text!

I hope you read me in my best self

Two and two make four,

One and one: two

But those three words you said,

We could make a million more; amour

Is this enough of what I said?

Or do we need to test,

It is for the best; say yes!

Sweet child

The sweet children of D'lore

In what a sinful world

Have you come

What brings you here

What do you want, child?

Says the Lord.

Dear Ella

Shining like moonlight;

Was her body bright?

Who could dim her light?

Neither the sun nor the moon,

Everyone knew.

That the lake was her favourite sight.

I hope to see you by the lake.

While I fish for hours,

Sing songs sweet,

And let my eyes rest;

Rest upon your calming spirit.

By the lake was a dense forest;

Here she feels safe,

The water nourished her body

The sun painted her soul

And I by the lake;

With her sweet glance, blessed!

Do you see the violets in the sky?

All the birds singing goodbye lullabies:

Leaving for home.

Sun drowning to give the earth relief,

Just the moonlight now,

And a cool breeze across my cheek.

Waiting patiently for the next day to seize;

All the goals and myself to please.

Looking around, beauty I see.

Even with eyes closed, I believe!

Fly li'l bird fly, nobody sees.

Cry li'l bird cry, always at ease.

It's such a short life;

Be yourself, please.

Look away

Far away

Far in time

What can you find?

Looking for a lost cause

Are you blind?

What sings the bird?

While asleep,

I hear you weep!

Dear li'l bird,

What songs do you sing?

Those sweet melodies;

Whom did you teach?

My heart melts;

With your warm voice!

Your whispers please all;

To those who hear!

Those still in bed,

How do you tease?

Still asleep,

and yet you, please!

Lil bird, how happy you fly,

Singing the songs of day and night.

Fish in the sea

I was at sea;

And what do I see?

A fish, there it is.

Is it breathing, or is it laughing?

Funny it is,

Is it swimming, or is it walking with fins?

Sometimes when I look,

I see them jumping into the sky!

Maybe air, they are missing!

Or is it water they are teasing?

Maybe they wanna fly,

Or is it birds they are feeling?

This late

You came this far

Rest your heart

Why so hurry

Are you getting late?

It rained gold yesterday

Seasons come by and leave as they please

Stopping amidst the chaos

Facing the tremendous heat of the sun,

Clouds fought their wrath to rumble and roar

The rain cries as if it hadn't shed its tears for ages

The dense forest finally got a proper shower

Its thirsty roots are satisfied.

Around some corner, I heard the toads pray for rain.

Birds sang out of the heat, searching for water sweet.

Following its nature, the sky rained;

To cleanse the mess of humanity:

The river's hustle and bustle, striking every piece of stone on its way to dust,

Carrying a gigantic weight on its back, challenging human creations and intellect.

The sun appears tomorrow

Rained continually for days,

and the clouds finally disappeared.

Happy sky; smiles its blues in bright

The warmth pierced my skin, melting my heart out,
rejoicing

Everything under it radiates new,

Fresh smells and fresh starts

It's been a long in the dark,

It's time to bloom, said the seed buried deep.

With each sprout opening its eye for the first time

Feeling overwhelmed, the sweet li'l plant grew
quickly until the next rain

Stronger day by day, grew the tree tall

Sometimes when I looked, a few birds sang there.

Oh! They built a nest too.

The next time I noticed, they were with kids.

Wait

I wait for the sunrise

A beautiful day to rise

The day I hear her, her sweet voice

The softness of her heart,

In her words, I'll feel, it'll fill me merry

I wait for her call, this day

Every minute today!

Oh! Like cool water!

On a hot day!

Will her melodies be;

To my heartache.

Birthday wishes

What do you seek?

It's your birthday, "Make a wish!"

Long life ahead, no need to speed.

You'll see all your desires are fulfilled.

Go on, "make a wish!"

Rising you shine,

Your soul is so bright.

May you outshine the darkness and lies.

Your path bright with all the stars

Glowing like an angel, you reach

We'll meet there, I promise.

All the laughter, joy, and times to enjoy.

Happy birthday to you again!

What a life!

What can you miss?

Wait

Let's wait a day.

One and two,

We pray

Nights

After a warm day came a chilling night

The sky filled with all its stars;

Under which I sat with me and myself

Silent mind trying to understand.

Open lips with sealed voices, breathing the luxury of living.

Universe trying to communicate, I said, I'm all ears

Suddenly everything stopped, and I began introspecting

Then I realised how everything made sense:

The past experiences were preparing me,

For the hardest battles yet to fight, for victories in life.

The demons inside me seemed undefeatable until I realised my power and believed in myself.

Now I've fought many battles of mind and heart

Finally turning me into an unstoppable warrior.

Sometimes we must hope and believe in ourselves with all the last pieces of patience.

Letting go of the things that weighed me down, I could move faster on my way.

Here I come

Far from you to go

The fears and tears

Left in the grave

No flowers nor memories

I pray

Here I come

To find my

Eternal peace

In this bliss,

Where we will feast.

Clock

On the wall

It hangs

The old, cute clock

Makes a round

Tick tick tock

The sun on her face

The green pastures,

Where she rests:

The sun; on her face,

Like the moon, she reflects.

The forest; green,

Makes her soul; seen.

Blue the sky;

Makes her wanna fly!

Fly, the little bird, fly!

Singing all your songs before night!

Hey sweet stranger!

Sing

Go sing

Sing me a song

full of melodies

Sweetness in the air;

It fills me with pleasure

The train of thoughts

Can I claim you? Tell me how?

Will you come to me to say it now?

Do you love me? Will you allow it?

Are you scared? Don't be afraid

You can trust me. Always remember that

Can we move ahead?

Or is it too late?

Is it too late to be more than just friends?

If I ask, will you give me your hand?

Will you be the mother of my children

Will you be my home, where I come to

Will you hold my hand when I am old and lonely

I want you to smile and be the reason for it

Will you be the friend of my youth and old age

Will you travel with me from city to village

If I am in trouble, will you rescue me?

If tomorrow never comes, will I be the first one on your mind

When I say I love you,

Will you repeat oh dear, I love you too

Lazy Sunday

I sing today

Today I write

No walks, no talks

I sleep today

All right

What is true love?

It's lovely seeing you shine,

It's dear to see your smile.

It's warm to see you near,

And I would love to see you here.

You glow like a diamond,

Your eyes; are blue than the ocean

Your heart soft as a rose

Where love does erose.

Hands, smooth as silk

Your hair, like a dense forest,

Keeps you so cool.

Your face, calm as the mountains

Voice, sweet like sugar,

In melodies, you speak.

If I could dive into your eyes,

If I could get lost in your hair

I would be amongst the luckiest men alive

Rage

Battling enough with self,

Now it's time to fight the evil of the world

Getting the right gear and training

What does it take?

How long will this go?

Whom to choose first?

Are you right, or just a better devil?

Who's with you?

Who are you?

Friend

How did it happen?

Where was it? We shared our first laughter.

Remind me; how was it like back then, the time we committed our first crime

Confusion of childhood, and mistakes of our teenage, does that only define us?

Or there is more to it, deep understanding, respect, and love for each other, dear friend!

Show me how you feel about me

Let's get crazy sometimes caring about each other's happiness like always.

The highs and lows of life are kinds of a hiking journey; let's hike on it together.

You do know! I got your back, right?

I know that you do too!

Why don't we ride through the tough roads toward happiness,

With a little bit of humour and some drama, aye?

So, when our grandchildren grow in our arms—we can share our masterpiece of a story.

Since this is the only life we get to choose.

Work

Born yesterday

I'm but one year old.

In this field of games,

I've come to learn and grow.

Happy birthday to you

I don't know how long it's been

Feels like a long time of connection between us

Every day,

I feel it even more.

I wish you a healthy and happy life ahead

You'll always be in my thoughts and prayers, I swear.

It's been a long time

Two years already.

Worst years without her,

It's been two days since we talked,

Two minutes since her thought.

Trying to forget her for the last two seconds,

It was the worst two seconds.

We are opposites in many ways,

It will not work, she says,

Slowly things were changing for the best.

Known her for two years back,

And never gone a few days without thinking of her,

Of what we could be.

Times lost and times gained

It was just a page when I started

It's been a few days since I was writing

Months turned into years

I grew up writing,

and getting old with this pen.

Now the writing remains of gold,

even when I'm old.

Good morning

Each day is special.

Special as you are,

Special, the way you are,

Yes! You are.

Somewhere between head and heart,

I'm choosing your smile.

Good night

Now you sleep! And the sun will rise to see you in the morning.

"What a beautiful thing to see after a long sleep."

That's what the sun says to the stars.

That's what stars gossip about.

Stars wait all day,

To see you at night,

To sneak through those windows.

They starve for your sweet glance,

What a beauty on earth!! Correct! says the sun,

"May the Lord keep her safe, warm, and healthy

So, we can come up every time,

just to see her beautiful smile,

Amazing eyes and good hair."

Says the moon as well.

Her! That gorgeous girl,

Sleeping beauty says all.

The ride

While we ride, everything just passes by.

Travelling through time, moments pass by with silent voices whispering like a breeze

I want to go,

Time in a hurry.

I want to stop,

 A moment to breathe.

Wanting to be in the present,

While I am thinking, it's a few seconds past.

Running between time,

Realising, after all, change is the only constant.

Lost

If I had left yesterday, I would be home today.

But I stayed to see the mess I had created

What a lovely day, they said.

Looking behind, oh! That's what I missed!

Promises

While the morning was bright

and happy for the day, we will meet again

In the afternoon,

 wept while waiting a long day

In the evening,

 the path clears of dust

Everything and everyone,

 welcome you and cheer you up

I hope you enjoy it all the way!

I wish for a blue sky once again.

Tomorrow

Your time will come,

The clouds will disappear,

The rain will stop,

And the fears last no more.

The sun shines brighter

Making your mood lighter,

The moon will be whiter,

and your smile wider.

The world is greener,

Our love grows deeper.

Our minds are generous,

Eyes see clearer.

Ears will hear louder

The bird sings sweeter,

The love grows wilder.

The rivers are calmer,

Which makes us remove our armour.

Happiness is in the air,

Freedom is everywhere.

A decision calling

We waited for days to make a call.

A call to decide our future.

A call that would change our lives forever.

I wish to talk to you all day long.

I want to miss you all the days gone.

Your smiling face

You smiled across the room like a full moon

Left alone like a forest in the dark

Nobody to look from far-far

Lost was a girl in the dark

With her light

She walks away for a sight

Lovely little girl, in the cruel night

Lost all hope

How could she fight?

But the lord sees,

He knows the truth, and the truth will guide her

She needn't fight for the evil is gone

With all the good done;

The bad still can't be outdone.

She can't outrun it! No.

But she can grow strong.

Darkness

No, I'm not afraid of the darkness

This madness can't infect my mind.

Beauty is everywhere

Beautiful mountains all around,

Still, why do I think of her?

Fresh air, everything new

Peace, calm here! Though I find in you.

What do I seek?

Is it love? Or is it you?

What makes my heart beat fast,

While I talk to you?

Is it true? You love me too?

How much do you do?

Tell me, why did you smile?

Why is that smile on your face

While you look at mine?

Why are you so lovely,

Shall I keep you? Now, do you mind?

Take me as your chair

Rest on me, baby

Come to me,

My heartbeat rests tonight.

Near my heart, she lives

The farthest of the land: there echoes my heart.

Floating like a bubble beneath the sea

What do I see?

At the very top, there is where she lives.

Head and heart

Cold my heart;

Seeks warmth of your love.

Head running wild;

Wants to rest here for a while.

Night

The night; long

Longing for someone, I sleep

May she come, I wish.

Wherever she be; she is well, pleases

6 ft Deep

Buried 6ft deep,

Delivered to Mother Earth;

In a beautiful box,

There's my body;

Ready to repeat the same cycles.

The cycle of life and death,

The cycle of love and pain is to no end.

A human life

Tormenting pain; left some on my brain.

Looking to clean it;

But no river, no sea!

What do I see?

Life and death:

What separates?

Fire in the sky

The big ball of fire:

Keeps me warm,

Lights my journey;

To mountains, rivers and everything to come.

All but pure desire to explore,

My heart out there cold,

Hey, ball of red!

Will you guide me till the end?

I'm in the shade

Will you be my sunshine,

In this rain?

Your life is precious

You don't have to live in pain

Your life is not in vain

Sweet dreams

Sweet sleep, baby sleeps

Your smile: baby's smile

Your laughter, like a rainbow after

Pleasant dream: the dream of me, of you

On a hill, mountain and caves

Hidden lakes, rivers and forest

Sweet babe on thy face,

I see a holy future traced!

Will you not rest: in your dream place?

After we collided

Like the rainbow after,

Like the moon after,

It's always the brightest of the stars,

That is seen!

So, glow with full power

I like you in that pink dress

The day after;

After we met,

All set on: a love quest,

Never rest,

No time breaks,

In a lovely place!

I wish to see you again;

Again, in a dreamy place.

I want to see you in that pretty dress.

Like rivers, my veins send love,

My heart; fills with your care,

In every touch, in every thought.

Let's meet again! Why not?

Fire in your soul

Push yourself, pray, and move, keep moving

Ahead is destiny, everything you ever wanted

There is a whole life ahead; why are you afraid

This is not how the story ends; it doesn't have to be like this

But it could be a new beginning and another adventure

You may rest a while, sleep as you need

Yes, you need to rest: for your body aches,

You have burned yourself.

Take it easy,

Be a tortoise, my friend;

Win with consistency;

Little progress each day!

When I looked at you!

The rain pouring,

My breath was warm, boiling the air

You stand there, Oh! A stunning view!

Sun shining, your smile so bright

I am in trouble; just breaking this ice

Are we different?

We are all different in some ways

And also similar to many

The only way to know ourselves is with,

Empathy, respect, and communication.

Life is the best teacher,

And we are the students.

It is this way we live.

Life nowadays has been sophisticated with conditionings!

That is what separates us; our conditioning.

All we want is a constantly happy life;

But it is the change; when we accept,

Happiness stays.

Dear mother

Mother, you are dear,

You were always there,

You thought best for me,

You fought for me,

You worked hard to build my future,

And you pray for better times ahead.

I may not say it often,

But there is no one like you other, mom.

There is Infinite love when you look up

It's bigger, it's better.

It's cool here,

It's dear and near.

It's the best feeling,

It's real. You need not fear.

It's love; it is for all.

Look closer, listen carefully,

and read between the lines,

You can have it; you can share it.

It's true, it's honest,

It's pure, with gentle care,

And it is yours.

Destiny

This is my life,

This is my fight.

Destiny is mine,

The time is mine.

I have to walk,

The path is mine.

Why cry?

Why be in the shade when the sun shines brightly?

Why be under an umbrella to enjoy the rain

Why not wear a coat while it's cold

Why cry when everything is fine

Why drown while you could swim somehow?

Why be alone when there are people around

Why be in the dark when there is a light

Why be in tears when there is no pain

Why be cold when it's warm inside

Why fail while winning is possible?

Why shut those eyes,

When could you dream with eyes wide open?

Why fight when you can forgive?

Why fall when it is the time to rise?

Without you

The earth is green,

The ocean is blue.

My life is dark

When I am without you.

I want you more

You are my heart,

You are my soul,

You are my freedom,

And I want some more.

Will you repeat?

Can you feel me, feel me near your heart?

Can you see me, see me through your heart

Will you hear me, hear me from your heart

Will you trust me, trust me for real?

Will you jump if I say I'll catch you?

Will you hold my hands when I say I'll never leave

Will you stop me, if I say goodbye

Will you hug me, if I say everything is fine

Could you make me laugh if I feel low

Could you make me asleep if I'm insomniac

Would you listen when I've something to say

Would you smile wide when I say,

" You look beautiful!"

Would you wink when I am bored

Would you hold me, if I fell

Could you calm me, if I panicked

Will you guide me when I am lost

Would you accept me as I am

Would you kiss me each morning?

Would you forgive me if I am late?

Could you love me till the very end?

Would you choose me if I want you forever?

Would you save me from every danger?

Would you be by my side in our old age

Will you do me as I do you?

Because I will, and I love you too.

The creator

I am green; I am the creator

Day and night,

The food and its fight,

The sun and its rays.

Call me thy father, thy mother,

And you can feel this love; this is heaven, sweet.

You can trust me

We are far, but I feel so near

Distance matters not!

Why should you fear

Please come here,

Give up on your worries,

Surrender those fears,

and let go of those tears!

You can trust me,

You're always near my heart.

A love song

You know I love you,

I'm crazy without you.

Come to me,

Say something.

You're the apple to my pie,

A colourful sky,

Laughter to my jokes,

All these smiles run miles

And I'll love you this way.

Will you be an umbrella for my rain?

Hey, good friend?

Will you be a blanket for my bed,

Butter for my bread?

I can hear your voice,

Even in your silence,

I can see it in your eyes,

I can read it on your lips,

You love me too.

Yes, it is you.

Now tell me you do!

A party song

Let's party,

Let us party tonight.

It's a beautiful night,

And we can dance the night.

Can you feel the music?

I can see your body move.

Can you feel the heat?

I can feel your heartbeat.

I know you got the moves,

Come now, show it.

It's a perfect night,

You're in the spotlight

Come on, baby, the party is on.

You can dance until sunrise,

and we can party all night.

It was blue

It is green here, but I feel so blue

It is bright as day, but I see only darkness

The sun is shining, but it is still cold

You are smiling, but I see your tears

You deny it, but I know.

You are lying, but I don't mind

You care, yet you won't show

You do love, and you're afraid to share.

I want to be with you, but it is raining.

The clouds are gone, and the sun is up

It's a new day to start over.

It's a perfect day to get together

It's now or never; this love is forever

A breakup song

The days are long,

Nights, lonely without you.

I miss you badly,

I want you by my side here.

Like a sweet melody,

You're on my mind.

I hope this time,

You don't mind.

I'll choose you every day

I want you through the day until midnight,

And text you good morning and good night,

I have all the good intentions,

You could throw all your tension.

A holy love story

I've been broken into pieces

Piece by piece, I collect myself

Fears stopped me,

The thoughts tortured me,

But your love is relaxing.

I thought I was the only one

But now I see myself in you.

My heart is out of control,

It beats only on your rhyme.

Why not love?

Do I leave, or shall I kiss

Tell me, how do I love you?

To make you miss me.

Teach me: how to get you nearby,

How to earn your trust?

How can I help you understand this love?

You are here

You will remain in my brain.

You may leave, but the memory lives.

You may forget, but I will always remember you.

You may not believe it, but I have always loved you

Let's be friends

We can be the best,
Beat the rest.

We can walk through the park,
Drive through the valley,

We can; watch the birds sing,
Count the stars on sleepless nights,
Dive through the sea,
And run through the forest deep.

We can go further,
Can go higher,
Go faster,

We can party,
Sing and dance,
And travel around the globe,
Come, let's explore!

There is magic in your love

I've seen it in your eyes,

Heard your whispers,

Read it on your lips

I can feel it in your heartbeat.

My ears are eager,

To hear those three words.

There may not be magic in these words,

But your love is truly magical.

And I love you

I know you are shy,

a little afraid to meet maybe,

Finally, when we met,

You are so happy, I see.

I have told you a thousand times,

No buts, no maybes.

This is love,

And we are making our love story.

While the moments went by

Don't you miss me,

While I feel so lonely.

Don't you love me?

When all I did was love you.

Don't you remember?

All the moments we had,

the feelings we shared.

We have the power

We can: Grow together,

We can: Learn more,

Can: Run faster,

Can: Do good; do better,

Live longer,

Work harder,

And be happy more than ever,

We can do it, do it together,

We can: Travel often,

See: closer,

Kiss: longer,

Feel: good,

Help: everyone,

And have everything.

Earthquake—a heartbreaking disaster

I have seen death so close, so nearby

I see people dying, running for their life

I feel the earth moving beneath my feet,

and I hear people crying out for help.

Never felt so weak and helpless before.

The buildings shook with terrifying sounds.

I prayed with my hands firm,

For the quake could only shake my feet,

not my spirit.

There was no transport, no communication,

And a scarcity of food.

Money and power,

nothing mattered at that instance.

The storm

Huge or insignificant,

Fast or slow,

Dangerous or not,

The storm may come,

And we need to face it head-on.

It is near; you can hear,

But you are strong;

Shouldn't fear.

Hold on,

It will pass too,

Just like the one before.

Quotes

Laughing a little, sharing some stories

Living more of this life

Planning from a to z, I'm still out of the alphabet.

It's little of what the eye sees,

More of what the soul feels

Losing you was the only way to find me.

I'm the story you will tell your children about.

I take what I want, and I want it all

1000 battles strong!

Chasing dreams, or die trying!

Uno, dos, tres, we don't make mistakes.

I'm dynamite, but you are afraid of a blast.

I prefer to face the storm rather than just hide away from it.

The sea, the waves, the calm breeze under the warmth of the sun, such a wonderful combination.

Everything happens for a reason, but love and friendships just happen!

Never ask for permission to be yourself, as the rain never asks before raining.

You will never know the mystery; the third is how it's supposed to be.

You may believe what you see but you must believe what you feel.

I am a thunderstorm,

and you are afraid of little rain.

Too many places, too little time.

Nature is the supreme truth.

If you think you are playing a game with me, know you are another character in this game.

"I am the maze of my own making."

My bleeding heart in your broken jar of promise

Our souls; are so bright, darkness goes trembling blind.